CAN'T GET TO SLEEP

POEMS
TO READ
AT BEDTIME

MARK BURGESS

CAN'T GET TO SLEEP

MAMMOTH

For Mum and Dad

By the author of
Feeling Beastly – Funny verse to read aloud

First published in Great Britain 1990
by Methuen Children's Books Ltd
Published 1991 by Mammoth
an imprint of Mandarin Paperbacks
Michelin House, 81 Fulham Road, London SW3 6RB

Mandarin is an imprint of the Octopus Publishing Group

Text & illustrations copyright © 1990 Mark Burgess

ISBN 0 7497 0416 0

A CIP catalogue record for this title
is available from the British Library

Printed in Great Britain
by Cox & Wyman Ltd, Reading, Berkshire

Contents

CAT NAPS

There in the sun a tom cat lies
Relaxed, asleep with tight-shut eyes.
A timid mouse steps lightly past,
Glad to head for home at last.
An eye half opens, ears are pricked,
Tom cat's ginger tail is flicked –
But that is all; the mouse is gone,
Safely home and cat sleeps on.

I DON'T WANT
TO GO TO BED

I don't want to go to bed,
I'd rather stay up late instead.
I wish you weren't quite so meticulous –
Bed at eight is quite ridiculous.
With lots of time still left today
Tomorrow is so far away.
There's still so much I haven't done,
Going to bed just isn't fun.
Look at the clock – it isn't late –
I'm just not going, so bed can wait!

All right, all right, don't get cross,
I'm going now, I know who's boss.
Look, I'm nearly halfway there –
My foot is on the bottom stair.
You'll come and read? You said you would.
You'd better or I won't be good.

BATHTIME

I love a bath,
I love a bath –
It is such jolly fun.
There's nothing like
A bath for laughs,
I'm always having one.
I like to splash,
I like to splosh
In water nice and hot.
I like to wash
And wash and wash –
I love it such a lot.
And when it's over
And I'm clean
It's really such a shame,
So out I go
And play with mud –
So I can bath again!

THIS BED IS TOO SMALL

This bed is too small,
I've grown too tall.
Look, a hole in the sheet –
To make room for my feet.

NEW PYJAMAS

New pyjamas
Go bananas
Run around and shout like llamas!

New pyjarmies
Like salamis
Down our legs and up our armies!

Crisp new pyjims
Flap like pigeons
Quack like ducks and squawk like chickens!

Brand new jimjams
Just like wigwams
Yours are small and mine are a big man's!

THE HAPPY HIGHWAYMAN

Long ago, in days of old,
When nights were very long,
There lived a happy highwayman,
The subject of this song.
His name was Thomas Turnip
And his fame had spread abroad.
The King had ordered his arrest
For thirty pence reward.

Now everywhere that Thomas went
He'd giggle and guffaw –
He'd laugh at anything at all
And roll about the floor.
He rode a fearsome horse of course,
Her name was Beastly Belle
And every joke that Thomas told,
The horse would laugh as well.

Tom rode around at dead of night
About the countryside.
He'd stop a passing coach and then
He'd take a peek inside.
Then he'd give a hearty shout,
He'd bellow loud and clear:
"Wake up, you load of nincompoops,
Did everybody hear?"

And thus he robbed them of their sleep,
These poor, well-meaning folk.
But Happy Tom would laugh and laugh,
Then tell some awful joke.
And then he'd ride away again
As quickly as he could –
Exactly why he did all this
Was never understood.

DAWN McHORN

Dawn McHorn is always yawning,
She yawns at night and in the morning.
She yawns at breakfast, lunch and tea,
She yawns for everyone to see.
Her yawning quite obscures her features
And when at school, she yawns at teachers.
And every question they ask Dawn
She always answers with a yawn.
All are agreed, it's quite appalling –
Dawn McHorn is ALWAYS yawning.

THE BAT

The batty bat sleeps upside down,
A funny thing to do.
I've never tried that way myself –
I wonder, p'rhaps, have you?

SNOW IN THE LAMPLIGHT

From my bedroom,
In bare feet,
I look through curtains,
Down the street
To the lamp-post
There below,
Lighting up
The falling snow.
Snow like feathers
In the light,
Like some gigantic
Pillow-fight.
Will it settle?
I'm hoping so.
Drifting,
Sledging,
Snowball snow.

KITTY KITTY

Kitty Kitty sang to the moon,
Kitty Kitty sang out of tune.
Though the Moon
Did wax and wain
Kitty did not sing again.

PROFESSOR ETCETERA

Professor Etcetera's earnest and wise,
He has grey hair, glasses and little blue eyes.
He spends all his time in research and in study
And he hardly goes out to see anybody.

He's studying sleep from all different angles.
He's working with sheets, pillowcases and
    mangles.
He's testing all sorts of alarm bells and clocks
And trying on nightcaps, slippers and socks.

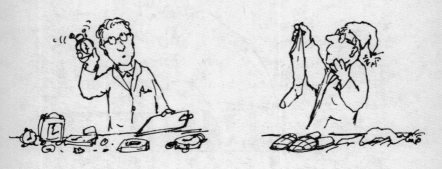

He's studying naps, forty winks and light dozes.
He's measuring snores from all sorts of noses.
He's bouncing on beds and testing their springs
And he's trying out quilts and duvets and things.

So hush, hush,
Do not disturb.
Quiet, please,
For surely you've heard?
The prof. is intent
On an experiment
AND NO ONE MUST UTTER A WORD!

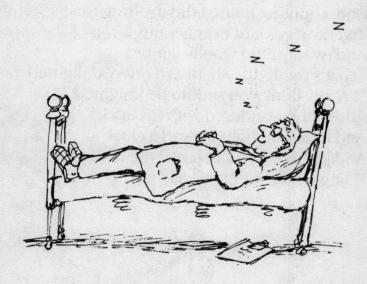

COUNTING SHEEP

As I was going off to sleep
I met a shepherd with his sheep.
The shepherd called me from my slumbers
And asked if I was good at numbers.
He said he had to check his stock
And wanted me to count his flock.
I soon agreed with his request
And, counting them, I did my best:
Twenty ewes and twenty rams
And twenty little woolly lambs.
"That's right," the shepherd cried, delighted.
"I really think you should be knighted."
And off he wandered with his flock.
And then I thought I heard a clock –
And just as they all reached the farm,
"Ding-a-ling" went my alarm.

27

IT'S JUST A JOLLY STORM

At night I like the jolly storm,
It is such fun to wonder
Just when the next big flash will come
And when the clap of thunder.
I like the pouring, pouring rain,
I like the flash of lightning.
It's only just a silly storm –
And nothing very frightening!

GOOD KING ROWLEY

Good King Rowley,
Rowley-Powley,
Went to bed
In bedsocks (holey).
The bedsocks (royal),
Did not spoil
As Good King Rowley
Put-them-on-slow-ly.

THE OWL'S BIRTHDAY PARTY

The Owl's Birthday Party
Is bound to be a hoot –
There's birthday cake and jelly
And coloured balloons to boot.

The bats are bringing chocolates
The squirrels, custard pies.
The birthday cake is full of worms,
The jelly's full of flies.

Everyone's invited,
We'll have a lot of fun.
The Owl really is a sport –
AND SO SAYS EVERYONE.

NOAH'S ARK

One stormy night, when all was dark,
The stormy waves beat round the Ark.
Hard on the roof the rain did fall –
Poor Noah could not sleep at all.
The noise outside was matched within,
There really was a frightful din.

Dogs barked
Warthogs called,
Bats squeaked
Cats caterwauled,
Elephants stamped
And tigers growled,
Hippos snorted
Wolves howled,
Parrots squawked
And monkeys chattered,
Donkeys brayed
And toads nattered.
But worst of all,
The rhino's snores
Shook and rattled all the doors.

Then, his cabin door flung wide,
Noah looked about and cried:
"Quiet, please – I'm all upset –
I haven't slept a wink as yet.
This awful noise has got to cease;
Please let's have a bit of peace!"

The beasts saw Noah's angry frown
And, all at once, they settled down.
Then, singing softly, they did try
To soothe him with a lullaby.
Gently into sleep he fell
And in the Ark then all was well.
Except, that is,
For *Noah's* snores
Which shook and rattled all the doors.

MIDNIGHT FEAST

I'm often hungry in the night,
I think how nice to have a bite.
So down the stairs I softly creep
While everyone is sound asleep.
And then I help myself to cheese,
A sandwich filled with mushy peas,
Or marmalade on buttered toast –
They're the things I like the most.
Then when I'm full and feel well fed
I creep upstairs and back to bed.
But in the morning, strange to tell,
At breakfast, I don't feel so well.

THE LONG-CASE CLOCK

Tick tock,
Tick tock,
Goes the long-case clock.
Standing tall
By the wall
In the main front hall.
And the rhymes
Of the chimes
Give signs of the times.
And right
In the night
At the strike of mid-night
From the base
Of the case
Peers a little grey face.

GRANDPA NEVER SLEEPS

Grandpa doesn't sleep at night,
He never sleeps a wink.
Instead he tinkers with the car
Or mends the kitchen sink.

Sometimes he picks the rhubarb
Or polishes the floor.
And other nights he's shopping
At the local all-night store.

Last night he papered half the hall
And built a garden shed.
But when the rest of us got up
He *didn't* go to bed.

I don't know how he does it,
He's always on the go.
Grandpa never sleeps AT ALL –
At least, I think that's so . . .

SANTA CLAUS GETS
THE WRONG NIGHT

One summertime, not long ago,
There was no ice, there was no snow,
But Santa, fast asleep one night,
Dreamt everywhere was snowy white.
It was (he dreamt) late in December –
A busy time for him, remember.

All of a sudden he awoke,
He grabbed his hat, he grabbed his cloak.
He stuffed some presents in his sack
And lifted it upon his back.
He called his reindeer, found his sleigh,
He harnessed them without delay
And then he urged them swiftly fly
Up into the starlit sky.

Soon after this they reach a house.
They landed, softly as a mouse
And Santa, with his bulging sack,
Headed for the chimney-stack.
Down the chimney he did go
And came out in the room below.
But then, his foot still on the grate,
Something made him hesitate.
The room was bare –
No decorations?
No Christmas greetings from relations?
No brightly coloured Christmas tree?
All this puzzled Mr C.
And worst of all – extremely shocking –
Nowhere could he find a stocking.

Then, all at once, there caught his eye
A calendar. The month: July.
Like lightning Santa saw his blunder.
Why, he didn't stop to wonder,
But needing no additional proof,
He dashed back up on to the roof.
He urged his reindeer to make haste –
Back across the sky they raced
And just before the hour of dawn
They landed on his own front lawn.
Santa went straight back to bed,
An awful throbbing in his head
And only later did he find
He'd left his Christmas sack behind.

SWEET DREAMS

Last night my dreams
Were of peppermint creams,
Of sherbet and coconut ice;
Of turkish delight
All ready to bite,
Of toffee and pink sugar mice.

The sky was all spangles
And candifloss tangles,
The moon was a bright lollipop.
Each hill was of candy
And flavoured with brandy
With a dollop of cream on the top.

The sea was of honey,
All lovely and runny –
The ships had liquorice sails.
And chocolate fish
Swam with a swish
By the sides of the marzipan whales.

While back on the land
By the soft sugar sand
Peppermint horses all pranced.
And bells of meringue
Cheerfully rang
As off to the morning I danced.

THE CUCUMBER TREE

The cucumber tree
Is a wonder to see,
It's a beautiful sight in the spring –
When birds of a feather
All gather together
Each morning and evening to sing.

But the greatest of wonders
Is the crop of cucumbers –
Each one has a luminous glow.
And monkeys pick bunches
To brighten their lunches
And see their way home in the snow.

THE PIGEONS ALL HAVE HOBNAIL BOOTS

The pigeons all have hobnail boots,
They dance with heavy tread.
All through the night they're on the tiles –
I hear them from my bed.

Perhaps they think they're Nureyev
Or maybe Fred Astaire,
But anyway I wish they'd go
And dance about elsewhere.

THE BADGER

Brock, Brock,
It's ten o'clock,
Time for your evening wander.
Through moonlight pace
With stripy face,
To woodlands over yonder.

But Brock, Brock,
At five o'clock,
End your night-time ramble.
Turn your tread
Towards your bed
Beneath the tangled bramble.

TWILIGHT IN THE PARK

It is twilight in the park
And the dogs begin to bark,
On their early evening walks they are bound.
So pug, poodle and Dalmatian,
Corgi, spaniel and Alsatian,
Together, they all love to run around.

For there's nothing like the gloaming
For a bit of canine roaming,
To meet and catch up on the latest news.
To sniff and pick at bones
Then be off back to their homes
To baskets by the fire and a snooze.

THE GREAT BED
OF WARE

Oh, there's none to compare
With the Great Bed of Ware.
It's so great
And ornate,
It's eleven foot square.
A delight,
It is right
At the top of the stair
And there's always
Plenty of room to spare.

It once slept a knight
And his horse and his squire,
A maid and her aunt
And a parish church choir,

A king and a queen
In their courtly attire,
And a butcher and baker
And wandering friar,

A blacksmith with coals
Still hot from his fire,
A gooseboy with geese
And the local Town Crier,

A cat and a mouse
And a hat-pin supplier
And a newly-wed couple
They all did admire.

For there's none to compare
With the Great Bed of Ware.
There's normally
Plenty of room to spare,
But that night
It fell right
To the foot of the stair
With a crash.
Now, alas,
It is under repair.

CAN'T GET TO SLEEP?

I can't get to sleep,
I've counted sheep –
It hasn't worked of course.
No forty winks,
Instead I think
Of mutton and mint sauce.

No better are pigs
All dancing jigs,
Or running through the woods.
Much worse are girls
With golden curls
And bright-red riding hoods.

I've counted flowers
For hours and hours,
I thought they'd do the trick –
But no such luck.
I'm really stuck
For something, please and quick.

I've closed my eyes,
I've tried and tried,
It's awful, I could weep –
I'm wide awake
For goodness sake –
I NEED MY BEAUTY SLEEP!

BEDTIME STORY

Now listen, child, before you sleep,
To this improving tale –
It's bound to make you grow up good,
I've never known it fail.
Have you finished fidgeting?
For if you have, then I'll begin.

There lived a girl, not long ago,
Her parents called her Jenny.
Her manners were the best in town
And talents, she had many.
What is it now? I thought I said
To bring some water up to bed.

Jenny loved to work and work.
She loved to go to school.
She always learnt her lessons well
And never broke a rule.
Goodness gracious, what is wrong?
Just settle down – Shall I go on?

Now Jenny met a lion one day,
But she knew what to do.
For Jenny, boldly, said to him:
'I'm not afraid of you.'
You have to go? Oh, surely not.
I think you'll like this bit a lot.

The lion really was impressed –
It went all meek and mild.
Such are the powers of a good,
Polite, well-mannered child.
I'll read some more? Just for a treat . . .?
How very odd, you've gone to sleep.

STARS

Up above, the stars are twinkling,
Hundreds, thousands,
Quite a sprinkling.
Just how many?
I've no inkling,
That's what little me is thinkling.

LETTER FROM THE LAND OF NOD

Dear Sir,

From our records, it seems
That, last night, when you called in your dreams,
You left behind proof
That you'd just lost a tooth
In the place where your pillow had been.

But then, it appears, you forgot
To claim your reward, which is odd.
So as due recompense
We enclose twenty pence.

Yours truly,

The Fairies of Nod.

IF I WERE A DORMOUSE

If I were a dormouse
I'd have a little warm house.
For I'd be sure to choose
Somewhere comfortable to snooze.
My bed would be just right
For a dreamy, sleepy night.
And if you should take a peep
I'd be sure to be asleep.

In Bed

Now we're ready,
Me and teddy.
Into bed
Our "Goodnights" said.
Night night,
Sleep tight,
Turn out the light.

Bed's the place I like to be –
Especially when my ted's with me.